George Mouse's Caravan

Heather S. Buchanan

Methuen Children's Books

George Mouse was excited. It was the middle of summer and he had decided to take his family away for a seaside holiday as a birthday treat for his mother. In secret George was busy making a gipsy caravan for them all to travel in. The caravan was to be pulled along by three mice, running between the shafts.

George lived with his parents and five sisters in a tree stump, and he had his own workshop under the roots. When he was working on secrets like the caravan, he would never let anyone come in.

He made wheels with spokes from logs, and bolted them together underneath a wooden frame, with twigs hammered across. He cut up an old tin can and beat the metal flat with his hammer. This he made into a little stove with a chimney.

He lit some logs inside the stove, and to be sure that it really worked, he secretly borrowed his mother's kettle and made a pot of acorn tea.

Next, he made bunk beds for all the family. Underneath these he fixed lots of drawers and cupboards in which to store food and pack away their towels and clothes. He hung little wooden mugs from a line of pegs near the stove. Over all this he put a roof made from an old plastic juice bottle which he had sawn in half. He nailed it on carefully, so that it could not blow away.

When the caravan was finished, George pulled it to a safe hiding place behind some buttercups. Then he called his sisters, Bryony, Campanula and Clover, to come and see it.

The girls spent the afternoon mixing paints made from different-coloured crushed berries and limestone powder. Then they painted wonderful gipsy patterns all over the caravan. They made their brushes from twigs and tufts of sheep's wool, which they found in the hedgerows and combed out with teasels.

Whilst their sisters were painting, Cowslip and Daisy sewed patchwork curtains from scraps they had collected: a lost silk headscarf, three handkerchiefs accidentally dropped along the riverbank, and even a picnic tablecloth which they had dragged to Tree Stump House. They used the fingers of an old woollen glove for sleeping bags. Daisy collected thistledown, and filled a cushion for each mouse, and they all stowed away buckets and spades and food in the cupboards. At last they were ready!

Next morning it was Midsummer Day, and their mother's birthday. As the dawn chorus began, they led her out to see her wonderful present. She peeped through the buttercups, and was so amazed by what she saw that she had to sit down for a moment. She was delighted, and very excited about going to the seaside.

George's father inspected the wheels carefully, to make sure that they were quite safe. Then the whole family scrambled inside, and each mouse chose a bunk bed.

The journey began. George linked paws with Clover and Campanula and they lifted the long yellow shafts, pulling the caravan smoothly along. It was hard work but they sang as they went. Everyone felt very happy.

At lunchtime they stopped by a farm gate. The younger sisters spread out a table-cloth for the picnic, while Campanula and Clover stretched out in the shade of a dandelion. Butterflies fluttered around. It was a lovely day and their mother said it was the best birthday she could remember. The girls had made a birthday pudding with apples and blackberries and honey, which was simply delicious.

George stood up and sniffed. At last he could smell the sea. They set off again, with Bryony and George's father helping to pull this time. As they topped the brow of a hill, they saw the sea. A great squeaking of hoorays rose from the caravan. They could hear the seagulls overhead, and Daisy jumped for joy.

They started to make their way down the cliffs towards the sand, but then things began to go wrong. The large wheels were turning much too fast and the mice felt the caravan running away with them. It took all George's strength to hold the shafts and he shouted at the others to wedge stones under the wheels. Only just in time did they manage to turn it sideways across the slope.

Campanula found a path which wound more slowly down the cliffs. George gently pulled the caravan down, whilst the others formed a chain and steadied the back wheels.

Once safely on the sand, they unpacked buckets and spades and changed into swimming costumes.

Tails flying, they scampered down to the
sea, and the first one in was George! They
swam and splashed, jumping over the
wavelets. Then they ran along the beach,
collecting wonderful shells and glossy
stones, polished by the sea.

As dusk fell, Father Mouse heaped up the pile of driftwood he had collected and lit a little fire. They sat around it in their towels and spread out their beach treasures, singing sea shanties and eating fish and seaweed stew. George had found a paper cup which tomorrow he would make into a boat. Now he was so sleepy that his eyes would not stay open. He wriggled down in his woolly sleeping bag and dreamed wonderful dreams, whilst the others planned games of cricket and expeditions for their holiday.